Stuck with a Bad Boy Billionaire

Billionaire

A GRUMPY ENEMY TO LOVERS ROMANCE

KASIA KAIN

Chapter Images: Pixaby.com/Prawny-1766270
Formatted by: Dawn Baca

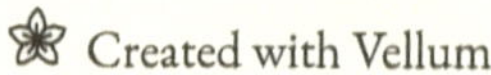 Created with Vellum

To my mom and dad...
You made me who I am.
You are missed every single day!

To my sister Jacqueline,
Thank you for always being there for me no matter
what. I couldn't have asked to be blessed with a better
sister and friend.
You truly are the best.

And to GOD.
Without you, I would not be.

Blurb

I let my guard down and my bad boy billionaire boss stepped right in

Dominic

I chose to stay away from everyone after I couldn't let go of my past mistakes.

Then, Mia walked into my life, and we were forced together by a hurricane.

She should fear me, but she doesn't. The sexual tension between us is fiery.

Oh, the things I want to do to her.

I want to hear her moan with excitement and pleasure her like she never has been before.

Mia

Trapped in the club with my boss, Dominic, he is so cocky... and so damn gorgeous.

I know I should fear him and run for my life, but I can't.

When he wraps his arms around me, I just melt.

He says he holds many secrets.

One he has never told anyone...

Until tonight.

It will change everything for us...

One

Hurricanes Here!

Mia

I wiped down the bar for the tenth time tonight, watching the storm outside. The wind has picked up speed in the past hour. I glance around the Miami Club, a sophisticated bar with extravagant lighting and decor, a counter for serving drinks, and an overall laid-back vibe. It's usually packed on a Saturday night, but the hurricane warnings have kept most of the regulars away. I sigh and look up when I hear the door open, surprised to see

Dominic Bentley, the club's owner, walking in. He reaches a strong hand up and smooths his dark hair into place. His dark brown eyes are intense and never miss the chance to lock onto mine. It used to intimidate me, but I'm used to it, now.

"Hurricane's close. Still going to spend your day upstairs?" I ask, half teasing and half criticizing him. I raise an eyebrow.

Dominic scoffs at me. "Why do you care?"

"Never mind." My voice, monotone, matches my true mood.

"Yep," he finally says, his voice low as he gestures towards the staircase that leads to his private apartment. "Came down to close up the bar for the day."

I nod and continue to clean glasses and adjust bottles of wine.

Dominic leans against the bar, watching me. His biceps push against the sleeves of his t-shirt. I gulp and look away. I've never let myself go there. Instead, he and I stay in the bounds of employee/boss very well. "You know, Mia, you don't have to be here. The storm's only going to get worse."

"I know," I say, ignoring the way his voice thrums through me when he says my name. "But I need the money."

Dominic snorts. "I pay you enough."

I roll my eyes and choose to focus on cleaning the table instead. Does this guy even know how arrogant he comes off, sometimes? He just assumes things without even asking. The truth is, I barely make ends meet.

We fall into silence, listening to the howling wind outside. I'm about to request that Dominic lets me work for a few hours more when the lights flicker and then go out entirely.

"Great," I mutter, reaching for my phone to use as a flashlight.

"Power's out," Dominic states the obvious.

His words get under my skin. As hot as he is, he is equally as annoying. "What are you going to do about it?"

He shrugs. "We'll have to wait it out. With all that rain, the roads are probably flooded already. And that wind out there will scoop you up like that." He snaps his fingers. I can feel his eyes rake across my body in the semi-darkness.

Nope, we don't go there.

I huff at him, folding my lean arms across my ample chest. "Great, just what I need. Stuck in here with you."

Dominic smirks. "Sorry to disappoint you, sweetheart." He doesn't look sorry at all.

I gaze at him. I can't stand his cocky attitude or when he makes me feel like he's looking down on me. It doesn't help that he is forty-seven and I am twenty-two. He's done well for himself, and I'm just starting out. I spot the expensive watch on his wrist and my eyes trail up his arm, leaving me completely distracted. I bet he always wears tight shirts with his sleeves rolled up so girls can ogle at his muscles. *Arrogant prick.*

We settle in at the bar, sipping on warm beer and making small talk. As the night goes on, the storm rages outside, and the winds are howling as the rain pounds against the windows.

We call each other out on little moments. He complains that I am suddenly lethargic at work and should work with enthusiasm. I defend myself by stating I earn my pay. He's called me out before, so I know he's trying to irritate me. Our barbs become squabbles.

It would be awful to make him my enemy right now just because we are both frustrated, so to diffuse the situation as well as to pass the time, I suggest we play a game.

"Games? Those are for kids," he scoffs, lifting muscled arms in a bored stretch.

"You have something better to do instead? Don't tell me you're scared," I chuckle.

"Fine." He immediately responds, as if I hurt his feelings.

I take an empty beer bottle, propping my phone against it, and use the flashlight on my phone for better visibility.

I explain to him the rules, and we begin to play a simple game of truth or dare.

He gives me multiple silly dares to complete, and I give as good as I take. I admit, it is fun to see him let loose a little. I finally fail to "chug a whole bottle of vodka."

"Kiss me," he says, a dare in his dark eyes. "That's the penalty I decided for failing. Those are the rules, right?"

His words make me laugh with a mix of surprise and curiosity.

Is he attracted to me, too?

But seriously, kiss him? I stare at him, sizing him up. I feel like I have him figured out. He wants to boost his ego and jab me back on the "scared" insult, knowing I will chicken out.

No, I can't let him have the upper hand. After all, it's just a kiss, right? I will give him a tiny peck on his full lips and prove my point. Nothing else.

I take him by surprise when I lean forward and give him a kiss. But once I start, I can't seem to back away.

Our kiss is electric, and his lips are so soft. I'd noticed he was hot before, but the way my body is responding to him takes me completely off guard. I breathe in his manly scent and feel his tongue gently brush against my lips.

He wants this, too. He wants me.

The thought sends shockwaves of desire through my brain. I always thought he was a bit out of my league, at least, financially. Well, physically, too. He is a *built* man.

"What are we doing?" I ask, my voice breathy.

Dominic leans into me, pressing his forehead against mine. "I don't know, but I can't stop thinking about you."

His breath is warm on my cheek, and I shiver. I linger for a moment, my mind numb with desire. And then I give in to the passion that's consuming us both. Before we know it, we're locked in a heated kiss. My lips part as his tongue finds his way into my mouth, dancing with mine. I moan and his hands grip my waist. I'm pulled off the barstool by the electricity sizzling between us. I press myself against him as his hands roam my body.

As the hurricane rages on outside, Dominic and I are caught in a different kind of storm that will change our lives... forever.

I feel a strong arm on my shoulder as Dominic pushes me against the wall.

"What are you doing?" I ask coyly, even though I know exactly where this is headed, and I like it.

"You know, this might be our only chance," he replies seductively, "to have hot... *very* hot... sex." He draws his words out slowly, lips still pressed to mine, and I feel warmth spread between my legs as my arousal increases. "What happens here in the bar, stays here."

It's like he read my mind, my fears. I can't afford to lose this job after a fling with the bar's owner. But in that moment, I *need* him. I need to give in to my desire. I have been pushing down my attraction to him for weeks and now, he consumes my every wanton thought. Even though I was exhausted and grumpy an hour ago, I want him to be in me. Now. He grabs a condom from his back pocket.

Convenient.

I smile as I ruffle his black hair, then I trace his sharp jawline, his beard and the scar just below his bottom lip with my fingers. His dark brown eyes are still piercing into me as he undoes his belt and loosens his pants. I want his muscled body—all of it.

Passion surges in me and I grasp his thick length as soon as it springs free of his boxer briefs. He grunts in approval. He is enjoying the fact that I am in command. I unbutton his shirt and move him, so his back is now against the wall. His dark eyes smolder at me.

I kiss and lick my way down his muscled torso and reach his happy trail. I lick his dick all the way to the tip with my tongue and then take his length into my eager mouth. He moans and raises his head, breathing faster. When I begin sucking, he wraps his thick fingers in my hair and gently thrusts his dick into my mouth, controlling the speed. His hands go under my shirt, and he unhooks my bra, revealing my full breasts. He fondles one of my pink nipples and I use my hand, looking up at him while I stroke him.

"My God, you're beautiful." His voice is hoarse, throaty.

He pulls me up, suddenly impatient, and unzips my pants, sliding a finger inside my panties to feel my wetness while his other hand basically rips my pants off me. My knees tremble and I feel his heat match mine as he towers over me.

I let my supple tits come in contact with the bare skin of his chest as his thumb massages my clit. With his free hand he glides his fingers down my neck and over my jaw till he reaches my breasts. I feel my plea-sure peaking, just from his thumb. He hooks a finger inside me, and I scream. Using the fingers of his other hand, he teases my nipples, making me moan with each touch. I can feel his hand moving down my body.

"You're so wet for me," he says against my lips.

"I'm going to come—don't stop," I breathe, my voice aggressive, my desire unleashed.

"Come for me, baby girl, before I take you." His voice sends me over the edge, and I let loose into the moment of bliss.

He gives me my moment before flipping me around, hands on the wall, his dick positioned just outside my wet folds. He rubs the tip against me and has me begging to be fucked. He chuckles and fondles my breasts as he enters me. I gasp at his size and beg for more. He is amazing and, in that moment, I feel like I never want this night to end. He takes me to the edge of pleasure twice before he is finished with me.

As he pulls out, condom full, I turn to face him. He kisses me like he wants me again, and I match his passion.

The rest of the night is a blur as we give into our cravings, eventually making our way up to his apartment and crashing into bed together.

My eyes open to the sound of thunder, and the feel of a strong arm wrapped around me. I snuggle into him, enjoying his warmth. I check my phone beside my pile of clothes. It is five in the morning. We crashed just a few hours before, but I'm not sleepy. As the minutes tick by, the storm outside persists, and I begin to realize we might be stuck here for a while. Dominic and I are huddled together for warmth, his body pressing against mine. I feel a surge of desire that I can't ignore.

I think about the night before, the way he explored my body as if he had been starving for it. Although it was sudden, deep down I know that I enjoyed it just as much as he did. It's too bad he owns the bar, and I am just an employee.

Logic kicks in as I realize the obvious. I just slept with my boss. Even if he didn't seem like a boss some-times, that's what he was. *Shit.* Did I just blow this job with my poor choices? He is successful and sexy, way out of my league. I don't think he's perfect, but he is definitely pulled together. That arrogance is part of what annoys me about him.

I decide to roll out of bed and get dressed. It is long past time that I try to find my way home. The ruffling of my clothes must have startled Dominic as he suddenly jolts up. He seems to be having the same mental processing as I am because he avoids my gaze. He quickly throws on some pants and starts to mutter.

"Powers still out, eh?" he says and checks his

phone. "No signal. We are stuck here for a day more, at least."

Stuck here for a day! I lock my gaze on him. He matches me, gaze for gaze, like a challenge. I can sense his jet-black eyes staring into my soul. I can also feel the pain hidden behind these eyes. When I first met Dominic, I became suspicious that there was more to him. I tried to figure him out, but he always cast me aside. But last night, when he was inside me, making the best love to me of my life, my suspicions molded into the truth because it's much harder to lie with your body than it is with your words. It felt like he wanted me with his entire soul, but he was afraid of me, too. The sex we had was intimate and that's why his eyes couldn't lie.

The darkness of the room has a haunting effect. As the reality and isolation of our situation closes in around me, I can't help but feel terrified. What if we are stuck here for more than a day? Hurricane season in Florida is no joke. Even if the storm stops, the damage afterwards is what can keep people home-bound until it's safe to go out. What if the storm is worse than we imagined? I start to hyperventilate a bit, and Dominic reaches out to stabilize me, pulling me to him. His warmth spreads all over me. His arms are big enough to wrap around my whole body.

"It's alright," he murmurs. "We'll wait it out. Don't worry. We will make it, together."

I start to mimic his comforting words. "We'll be ok. We will make it," I assure myself, my voice surprisingly quiet. "All we can do is keep each other company until the storm passes."

As Dominic and I stand there, trapped in the bar, I can't help but feel conflicted. I am grateful for his company; if I had been alone during the storm, I would have been a mess. But on the other hand, I can't shake the feeling that something isn't right.

I start to doze off, thinking about all the stools and tables that need cleaning and all the different bottles of alcohol that need to be arranged.

Two

Let's Not Talk About It

Dominic

Mia and I are still holed up inside the Miami Club even though the storm has been roaring for hours. The power is back on, but the storm's other effects, including the wind and the rain, are not letting up. Although we severely lack entertainment, we nevertheless find a method to keep each other diverted despite the predicament.

"Thank God, the light is back on," Mia sighs.

"Although I liked your face better in the dark," she taunts. I'm glad to see she's back to her normal self. Her panic attack earlier concerned me. I know I'll do everything I can to protect her.

"Mmm, I bet you like the dark from now on." It takes a moment for her to process my jab, but when she does, her face flares a pretty shade of pink, and she tries to hide it.

"Let's not talk about what happened last night, shall we?" she says sheepishly, her eyes cold. I watch her pick at the fabric of her jeans, the same ones I ripped off of her last night. I feel my cock twitch in desire, but I clamp down on my memories.

I realize that I am opening myself to Mia in a way that I have never done before as we are sitting on the couch together in the corner of the club. If it had just been a one-night stand, then I'd be avoiding her, wishing she could go home so I could be alone. But I don't want her to go. I enjoy her company.

"So, how did you become the owner of this huge club?" she asks while checking her phone. I can tell she is desperate for help, but I already know there will still be no sign of it until the storm passes. I decide to distract her from her anxiety the best I can. The selfish part of me wishes I could hold her close and make love to her again, even if she is acting like last night never happened.

I clear my throat and say, "I can't take all the credit for my success. I grew up in huge mansions. My family's got some fairly large assets in New York City and investments that have paid off well. Living the high life as a teenager definitely left a mark on me. New York is where I was born and raised, but I had to learn to be independent early on because my folks were always busy with work. So, I had to figure out how to take care of myself, you know what I mean? Part of that was building my own wealth. This club was my first successful venture, and that's why I stay here. My other properties are managed by a firm."

I can see my words make her feel small because she shrinks a little on the couch. Instantly, I feel bad. I switch back to talking about my teenage years, a topic I always keep to myself. I tell her, "I never had any real friends." And I am being truthful. I described the guys as "just a bunch of hangers-on that wanted to be near the money my parents had."

"So, why didn't you stay? With your parents, I mean. It seems to me you had everything," Mia says, her beautiful eyes full of sympathy. My heart swells at her naivety. I imagine how much she would detest me if she knew the real me, or at least, who I used to be.

She is so pure, and I'm drawn to that like a moth to a flame.

"Money isn't everything, Mia," I say softly. "I was a child back then, and I needed my family, their attention, but instead, I was showered with... wealth. Some people might think I was lucky, I guess. But your father not being with you half of the time, friends near you for your money, people judging you unfairly purely by what your family has, the 'I love you, and your wealth' takes a huge toll on your brain as time moves on. I started to do really messed up stuff back then, which I have left behind, things that could kill." I regain my composure and realize what I was just about to say. I quickly try to change the subject. If she knew, she'd be looking at me with disgust, not the desire I saw in her eyes last night.

"That could kill your creativity," I save myself. "Anyways, you know what's more powerful than capital? Connections, Mia."

Mia pays close attention as she listens, and the icy blue of her gaze gradually softens. "It seems as if you've been alone a lot."

I manage to stifle a sigh of disappointment as I say, "I was. On the positive side, I could fend for myself once I reached that point. And when I got to the point in my life where I could make my own choices, I made the conscious decision to carve my own path. This is how I ended up owning this club in Miami, and I couldn't be more grateful."

Mia indicates her approval with a small nod, and I can see the gears turning in her mind. She says, "I see. That's the key to your tremendous success." She offers me a smile.

I shrug. "There was some degree of luck involved in the undertaking. As I said, I did really, let's say, unlawful things back in the day. But in response to your question, the short answer is, yeah, you probably could say I've done rather well for myself."

I want to reach out and touch her cheek with my hand, stroking her chin with my thumb, but I resist the urge and clear my throat. "And what exactly can I say about you? You're a mystery yourself." I am curious and looking forward to shifting the subject, so I settle back into the couch. "Walk me through your past."

Mia briefly pauses, during which time it seems as if she is considering whether or not to share. But, after taking a few long, deep breaths, she then begins to recount what has happened.

"I was raised in a quaint community in the middle of a small town by a single mother. I was an only child. It was difficult for my mother to provide for both of us simultaneously. I..." Her voice chokes up. "I was really malnourished, you know. It was bad. Making friends was difficult, and I was bullied at school because of my clothes and for not having the money to do sports or... anything, really. My family's financial status wasn't exactly a secret in a town that small. But luckily, I was really bright, and I still am. My grades were always on top, allowing me to get a scholarship to a small college and, eventually, get a job." she says and smiles happily.

I now understand why she had a painful look in her big, blue eyes when I talked about my wealthy upbringing. I wonder if she's still paying off the loans she would have needed to take out for her undergraduate degree, even with a scholarship. I felt bad for teasing her about her money the day before.

She speaks with a look of stubborn determination in her eyes as she remarks, "But I've always known I was made for much more," she says. "I decided to relocate to Miami so that I could establish a better life for myself. This job gives me flexibility and after a few years of experience, I want a corporate job somewhere... with lots of benefits." She wrinkles her nose at me, and I laugh. The benefits of working at a bar aren't great, I know.

Her backstory took me entirely by surprise. After hearing about Mia's history, I am even more attracted to her. Her consistency in showing up for her shifts and taking other people's shifts makes more sense, now. I'm confident that she is a brave and independent young lady. Her past has completely sold me on the fact that she has grit and determination.

Exactly what I want in a wife. The thought swirls in my brain so fast that I can't stop it. My breath hitches in my throat and I cough.

Immediately, Mia is on her feet, going to grab a bottle of water for me. Our hands brush as she gives it to me. One look in her eyes lets me know she wants me again, and I want her, too. But not yet. We have too much to learn about each other, first. Plus, I'm not exactly a free man. I need to be careful.

We continue talking off and, on all day, and far into the night, exchanging stories with one another and getting to know each other in a way we have not done before. I can't help but feel more and more drawn to her. Mia is a natural beauty with her heart-shaped face, high cheekbones and a button nose. She has full lips and sultry eyes. Mia's long hair is a rich chestnut brown and flows down to her back. Her messy bun she wears to work gives her a carefree look. I cannot stop myself as if the cold, stormy night has attracted me to this flame, to her warmth, like a starving man to a gourmet meal.

I know I should stay away and not devour her

sweetness again. It'll only hurt us both when it can't go anywhere after. But I can't help myself. I need to have her again.

I take her by surprise and kiss her. Her soft lips send a shiver down my spine, and she starts to hold the kiss for a little longer. My hands begin to caress her breasts, and I can feel her nipples getting hard. Mia grabs at me desperately, arms around my neck. I begin to sink to my knees beside her and fumble with her panties. I stroke her with skilled fingers, and then with my talented tongue. I kiss between her legs, rubbing, nudging, poking, in a rhythm like a giant pulse. Her legs twine about my head and shoulders desperately. She is beginning to buck her hips, starting to come so quickly and deftly as if I have practiced such a maneuver many times with her. I shift my position to crouch over her. I let the moment be about her and pull back after she climaxes. To be honest, I'm feeling conflicted.

Despite our natural chemistry and hungry desire, I have to make myself stay aware that I need to exercise caution. In addition to my shady past, I am much older than her and have more money than she does, both now and in her past. Our ways of living couldn't have been more unlike one another. I can't allow myself to get too connected. She's just starting out in life, and

I'm well-established. Plus, she doesn't know the real me.

"We're not going anywhere for a while," I say, rubbing her arm lightly. She has pulled her pants back up and lounges against the couch, relaxed. "Might as well make the best of it."

Mia nods and nudges me with her foot as if to say, *we definitely are making the best of it*, but I can see the worry in her eyes. "I'm sorry," I say, feeling guilty. "This is all my fault. You wouldn't be stuck here if I hadn't shown up unannounced."

Mia shakes her head, sitting up. "Don't be ridiculous. I wasn't planning to leave my shift early yesterday. You don't control the weather. And honestly, I'm glad you're here. It's been... nice getting to know you better."

I feel my heart swell with warmth at her words. "Same here," I say softly.

We share a comfortable silence when my stomach growls louder than the storm, reminding us of our predicament.

"I'm famished," I say, standing up. "There is a vending machine in the back. Let's see if we can scrounge up some food."

Mia follows me into the club's rear room, where

we see the vending machine buzzing with noise. I dig through my pockets for some coins.

I feel my whole-body sizzle for Mia as we munch on stale chips and candy bars. She looks so sweet sitting there eating crappy food and not complaining. I smile to myself. For better or worse, we were in this together.

Three

The Art of It

Mia

I can't believe I just spread my legs for my boss...
again. This time, it was all about me, and I loved
it. I feel comfortable around him and, somehow,
I trust him. I know he's hiding something from me,
still, and I wish he'd just come clean to me.

Dominic and I settle into a nice rhythm of sharing
and laughing, keeping the conversation light. We
continue to share some past stories that make us
vulnerable toward each other, but nothing too heavy

has come up, yet. I spare him the details of my poor childhood, only making the occasional joke about it here and there. Sharing laughter attracts us to each other. I am also drawn toward him, and this is the first time that I am not willing to resist my feelings that are getting intense for him. I can't help but wonder how he will be in the broad light of day once the storm is over. Will he retreat into his shell and look down on me even more, knowing where I come from? I hope not. I know we are so different, and getting into this kind of attraction is not good but having him in front of me makes it so that I couldn't ignore my attraction if my life depended on it.

I feel confused because I never open up to someone this way. And I've been working for him for months and never had to battle my feelings the way I am now. Maybe the weather and the situation have made us available to each other and that is why we keep getting physical together. I can't believe a guy like him who has access to all the pretty socialites in NYC would actually want me. It's crazy.

I find myself opening up to him and I share some life lessons I learned when I was younger. I tell him how I wanted to become an artist and how that seemingly unrealistic dream changed me through the different ups and downs of my youth.

I share with him that I am passionate about painting and creating art pieces. I tell him that one of the rooms in my apartment has so many of my own pieces that I no longer name them. Instead, they are numbered. That elicits a chuckle from him. I blush and tell him that I imagine they are on display not in my own home but in the homes of other people, my fans. I even tell him what I do on my days off—I visit some of the galleries and to get inspiration for my art. I admit I haven't had an opportunity to bring my pieces to a show, yet. But one day, I will. First, though, I want the stability of a corporate job to be able to save up money, help my mom out, and build my retirement fund. I can't deny that a lot of my sparkle dies out at my proclamation. But I don't care. I grew up poor and I can't let myself be poor ever again.

He sits there and lets me talk, listening intently and occasionally reaching out to stroke my arm gently. Dominic shakes his head when I proclaim I want to get a corporate job. I know he doesn't think I'll be happy there. He tells me he knows someone who can take my pieces to be a part of an art exhibition, as he has connections with a local gallery owner. This makes me feel so happy because it has been my biggest dream in life. I thank him for providing me with such an opportunity, gushing at him with enthusiasm.

He holds my hand and says, "Anything for you."

His words send a shockwave of desire through me. I can't believe he's acting like he wants me. I want to ask him how he feels but am afraid to dig too deeply into his motives. He holds my hand more tightly, which grows a sense of intense sexual attraction between us.

Desire flares hot and bright in his eyes. He moves a little closer, holding my hand and trying to pull my face towards his with one of his hands. He places a kiss on my lips and tries to get more intense. I move towards him as thoughts of doubt and "shoulds" fade away in an instant. I take a deep breath and suck his lips; his beard brushes on my face as our tongues tease each other.

He gives one more deep kiss. He is sucking my lips so hard that I can feel a little pain, but I do not resist. I move my hand to his face to make the kiss more passionate and intense.

I love the way he smells and the way he tastes. All thoughts of reason leave me, and I hunger for him. His sucking increases my desire, and I lift my arms so that he can get my shirt off easily. He tries to pull it off and rub his body with mine. I can feel his warm body which makes me feel his want of me. After placing several kisses everywhere on my body, he moves up toward my face. He presses against my body so that I feel his hard cock and know how much I'm wanted.

I let that dream settle into my mind. *I'm wanted.* This successful, rich man wants me. The thought thrills me.

I take deep breaths as my arousal intensifies. His dick is massive, and he rubs it against my jeans between my legs. I try to move my hand to his cock to release it from his sweatpants. I want to feel its length in my mouth again. "How are you feeling?" he asks.

"I want you to fuck me." I hold his gaze, enjoying the way he is undressing me with his eyes.

"I want to make you feel so good, baby girl," he whispers, sliding his fingers into the waistband of my pants. I shiver at his touch. I love the nickname he uses for me during sex. Part of me wishes circumstances were different so he could call me his baby girl all the time.

Our clothes find their way to the floor and he moves me up onto him, letting me straddle him on the couch.

"Take that cock and show it who's boss," he teases me.

He places a kiss on my lips and I slowly sink my wet pussy down onto his rock-hard dick. He rubs my sensitive nub while I rock back and forth on him, my hand on his muscled chest for support. I lock eyes with him as I ride him, relishing the power I have over him in that moment. I watch as waves of pleasure wash over him.

He grips my hips and guides my rhythm. I bend forward and command his mouth to mine. Our lips crash into each other before I pull back to watch him near his climax.

"You feel so good. Yes, just keep doing that, baby girl," he says between gritted teeth as he tries to extend his pleasure.

Then, it gets to be too much, and his hips start to buck up, matching my speed. His breathing quickens and the look on his face turns desperate. I turn my focus on my own pleasure and move in ways that feel the best to me. All at once we come in a moment of panting and shuddering as all of our nerve endings come alive.

I'm not sure what it means that we can't keep our hands off of each other, but I am loving every minute of the connection we have. Especially since I know it won't last forever.

Although I am attracted to him physically, that nagging thought of reality tries to remind me that not only do both of us have a big age difference, his past is totally different from mine.

I steal away upstairs for a moment alone and to take a quick shower. I swipe a pair of his sweatpants and an oversized t-shirt when I'm done. As I descend the stairs, I can feel his steamy gaze taking me in with satisfaction. The shadows behind his eyes seem less intense, now. I know he wants me.

Instead, we resist our desire and play darts for a while. The dart board is a favorite with the locals and I'm not half bad at it.

We throw in silence at first. I can tell he's working up the courage to tell me something. My heart drops when he suddenly starts to share more about his life. He avoids my gaze and kind of just blurts out some things about his past. I can tell he's ashamed. It's so shocking, all I can do is listen and try to act normal.

My mind is racing but I try to absorb what he's saying. He was affiliated with a gang whose hitmen take money in return for injuring or killing people. He says that he is still affiliated with them and if he does not keep in touch with them, they threaten to kill him. They send one of their muscle men to check on him sometimes, mainly to remind him that they still remember who he is and where he lives.

I gasp. I know exactly the two men they send. They don't fit in in a bar like the Miami Club. They look rough, and seedy. Looking at Dominic's sexy body and smooth demeanor, I can't imagine him in a street gang.

I watch his lean body move as he hikes his arm back and arcs a dart through the air and onto the bull's eye.

"I never miss the mark with the things I really want," he says and winks at me, but his eyes are serious.

Is he putting a feeler out to see if I want him, too, beyond just right now? I pause and take a long drink from my water bottle. In this situation, after hearing his confession just and after having sex with him and getting to know him, I do want to know how serious he is, or isn't, about me.

He puts the darts back in their holder by the bar, placing each one intentionally, giving us both time to process. "Tonight was fun, wasn't it?" he asks me, his dark eyes probing my face, searching for a reaction.

"I never knew you could actually be both hot and... interesting," I tease him.

"Well, we can thank the weather gods for making things so good for us," he says with a smile. I can tell he wants to be close to me by the way he keeps looking at me, as if asking if I still want him, too.

"Maybe we should ask the weather gods if they're done, for now," I say, cocking my head to the side and noticing the silence outdoors.

He notices the change in my voice. I look at him to say something but choose to be quiet. My feelings are all over the place and I don't know which one to choose—the part that wants to stay with him and explore our connection or the part that wants to go far away.

"Hey, it's okay. You can tell me what's on your mind." He looks resigned, as if he already knows.

"Don't you feel that things shouldn't really continue... with us?" I ask him, flipping my hair over my shoulder nervously.

"What do you mean?" he asks gently, moving closer to me.

"I mean, that this isn't the right thing," I say, and then after a few moments, add, "I mean, like our age difference and... everything. I mean, you are my boss." I smile a bit sheepishly while looking at him.

He looks relieved by the reasons I give him and it's then that I realize how self-conscious he is about his street gang affiliation. I see him a little differently, now. Maybe he and I aren't as mismatched as I thought. We both have shame around parts of our past.

"I know this is a little... unconventional, Mia. And I've thought about the age difference, too." He sighs. "I really don't want to tie you down when you have your whole life ahead of you. Plus, I've made some pretty big mistakes."

The way he says it makes me yearn for him. I reach out to take his strong, warm hand in my own small one.

"I see potential here. And I'd never do anything to hurt you. That I can promise." His voice thrums through me, comforting me.

I nod and hold his gaze. I have no idea how our connection will fit into my life, or my goals, and I'm still not sure how compatible we are.

"I know that there is a big age difference and maybe a big difference in lifestyles as well, but I am a man of my word," he says, and smiles as I relax a bit.

He makes me believe that things are going to be okay. But I haven't been in a serious relationship, yet. Do I want him to be my first?

As if sensing I need a little space he stands up and walks to the door of the club. "I think the storm gods are done, for now." He casts a teasing look over his broad shoulder and I can't help but smile. He has broken the tension from our conversation and I'm glad.

Gone is that horrendous condescending look he used to give me. So many things have changed so quickly.

Although he tries to make me feel that everything is fine, I cannot deny a few thoughts that are the reason for making me feel conflicted. We've been in our own little bubble the past forty-eight hours, but with the storm dying down and the real world rushing back in, I feel more confused than ever.

He swings the front door open and a waft of humid Florida air spills into the room. He grins and tells me that the storm is over with no visible damage to the property. I get his meaning. I can now leave for home. My mind is racing. I feel afraid that if I walk out that door everything will be different between us. Will he think I was a mistake? Will things be weird at work, now? He tries to tell me once more that things are going to be fine and that I can trust him. I barely feel the kiss he plants on my lips as I stand at the door, minutes later, my handbag slung over my shoulder.

He offers to drive me home, but I shake my head and pull out my car keys. I can feel my walls rising up to protect my emotions and I'm powerless to stop them. I move outside and open my car door, looking back at Dominic. He waves his hand and smiles. He stands there, protectively, watching me as I drive away.

Four

Tell Me All of Your Secrets

Dominic

I've never been this way before. I am not open to people the way I was sharing things with her. It feels like the bond between us is a great, old one, and I can say anything I want to in front of her without fear of being judged or anything. Maybe the nights we spent together are the reason I was open towards her; that storm put us together. I get a chance to be vulnerable in front of someone I'm starting to really care about. I'm not sure she really understood the severity of potential consequences with my gang affiliation. Would she still want me if she knew how much my affiliation would hurt her reputation, and herself, if they got angry at me?

Having her with me during the storm made me feel a little lighter from all the fears and scariest parts of my life. The best thing about her is that she heard all those tough and bad times without saying a single bad word about me. She was perfect, sitting the whole night with a person like me, who has such a shady past.

It just feels good to be around her, and it's admirable on her part that she continues to listen and console me about my past. I tell her that there are a few things that are still a secret because telling these types of secrets can lead to my death. I can tell she sees how heavy the burden is that I'm carrying. I've already told her a few things. I want to tell her more, to just be out with it and know that there is another living being out there in the world who knows me to the fullest and still... wants me. *Loves me*, my mind says.

Of course, she asks what secrets I'm talking about. I knew she would. I wanted her to, even. She gets more than a little uncomfortable and scared when I tell her how high the stakes are and if I violate certain agreements, the gang leader will kill me.

But she doesn't leave or move away. She stays and

tries to comfort me. I feel my heart warm up to her, then. I know I'm falling for her, but I can't let myself. She'll end up getting hurt. The gang's clutches are still in me and that's dangerous. I squeeze her hand when she reminds me that I'm on the straight and narrow path now and that the past is far behind me. Hearing her share her heart like that, and seeing her belief in me, makes me feel that she is beautiful from the inside out. She makes me feel that there is something good left in me. I hold her hand and thank her for making me feel that I am living again.

She smiles and encourages me to get it all off my chest.

"No more secrets," she says, her eyes inviting me in.

I decide to tell her one of my deepest secrets from my gang days. If the group that I am still affiliated with, to some extent, got the news that I know the place where a woman liquidated her assets, bought gold, and then buried it, they'd torture me to take it for themselves. This gold she stashed away is worth a fortune. Mia's eyes widen.

I've been out of the gang too long to know for sure if they even remember the stash at all. I don't even know if it's still buried where it once was. I don't want Mia to think my role was the muscle, the ones with the guns, so I tell her the truth. I was running point for the gang. I was the eyes and ears that found lucrative opportunities. Most people think gang members just want power. But that's not true. Money, gold, valuables—that is what matters. I never hurt anyone, but my findings led to other people getting hurt, all the same. I feel I will never live down the shame.

Somehow, the woman with the gold ended up dead. The head of the gang thought that his brother was behind it, and he killed his brother for not being loyal. This created more issues for me because I knew if the leader learns about the fact that I personally played point for this caper, he will turn his irrational blame game on me, hunt me down, and torture me. I don't know any information beyond where her gold was once buried. So, I know he'd end up killing me.

"How on earth did you get out? Of the gang, I mean?" Mia's voice is small.

"I asked the gang to allow me to go, and I made a blood oath, promising to keep things secret. I wanted to go clean, as sometimes happens. For the moment I'm probably safe. But as soon as the lady and her money come up, I have a target on my back. I'm not worth much to them anymore. They just don't want me to talk. And I haven't. I'm no snitch."

Mia looks at me with her big, beautiful eyes and

just asks me one thing, and that is why I am telling all this to her. Why do I trust her when she could use all this information to harm me and extract money from me? Listening to her, I smile at her innocence and whisper to her how much I do trust her.

We made a few jokes here and there after I dumped my past on her to lighten the mood. I felt bad. Here I was a grown man still paying my dues to a gang I was a member of decades ago. I felt pathetic. Under my smile, I was worried she was judging me inside her mind. When she mentioned the storm had stopped, my heart had dropped. Our safe little bubble was about to be burst by real life.

It was so hard for me to let her go home after the storm ended. I knew I had to, but I was afraid she'd change her mind about me, once she thought things through. All I could do was stand there and watch her drive away, hoping she'd be back for work on her next shift.

Five

The Date

Dominic

Mia came to work today right on time. I could tell she was a little hesitant to see me. She looked impossibly cute in her jeans and branded t-shirt, the bar's logo on the front of it. She set her bag down behind the bar and turned to face me. As soon as I saw the soft look in her eyes, I knew everything was okay. She seemed to be unsure what I wanted from her. Was she afraid she was just a one-night stand to me?

.   .   .

I approached her and brushed a stray piece of hair out of her eyes, my hand lingering on her cheek.

"Hi," she said a little shyly, a small smile on her face.

"Hi, baby girl," I teased her and laughed as she blushed.

She swatted at my arm as punishment and laughed at me. "Baby girl, huh?"

"You know you like it." I watched as she readied the bar for our first customers.

"Hey, so, yesterday, when I told you everything about me, Mia, my heart felt so much lighter. I never dared tell anyone about my past. Not because I am scared but because of the people I am associated with."

.   .   .

She paused in her busy work and landed those blue eyes on me, patiently waiting for me to get to my point. I knew in that moment I'd do anything to keep her safe. I wanted more than just sex with her. I wanted all of her.

"Those people hold grudges. They do not move on; they do not like to forget. I hid from everyone. I hid under my bad-boy persona so that my past wouldn't scar someone."

A hint of a smile brushed across her face. "I'm glad to know it was just a persona and not the real you." She closed the distance between us and wrapped her arms around my waist, surprising me. "I believe in you, no matter what you've done before. I believe in a fresh start."

I kissed her forehead, enjoying the sweet moment. "The past is full of stupid and dangerous decisions," I whispered into her hair. "The past will not think twice before coming back and causing trouble. That is why I choose to hide it. I thought I was going to hide from everyone and live my life alone, but then came you, Mia. The pretty bartender who is like a breath of fresh air to me."

"Am I, now?" she asked softly, nudging me with her hips against mine.

"You are so brave. You know all of me and you're not afraid. You're still here. I didn't think it was possible. But I shared my secret past with you, and when you looked at me with those eyes, I could not help myself. Your proximity made me talk all about it. The nights we spent together were out of this world. I have dated here and there, but nobody has touched me like you, Mia. No one had this effect on me." I can see her melting at my words, and I pull her close to me, wrapping my arms around her tighter.

I am very attracted to Mia, but I am not sure if she feels the same. After all, Mia is young, ambitious, and beautiful. She does not need a man whose past is scary, or evil, and maybe she wants someone who is the same age as her. Maybe she wants someone fun or someone sweet and cheesy. I am not any of that.

"I believe in you, Dom." Her blue gaze pierces mine. I see sincerity in their depths. She pauses and then continues, a shy smile on her face, "I believe in us."

With that small admission, I am undone. She does want me. I scoop her up in my arms and twirl her around, the happiest man in the world.

"Date me, Mia. Let's give this an honest chance."

"Yes, let's." Her eyes sparkle up at me and I see forever in their shine.

* * *

After Mia stayed with me during the storm and didn't run away, she also made me confront my fears. I realized that I could not imagine my life without her. It does not matter that I am scarred, a little bit jaded, or a lot older than her. What matters are my feelings and the intentions I have toward her. I was elated when she agreed to let me date her. And today, I am taking her on our first date. I have planned everything. I am going to surprise her with her favorite things. She showed up for work as usual but I asked her to go back home and get ready as we are going somewhere, and I want to keep it a surprise. I almost lost my courage. I'm glad I didn't. Now I am in my bathroom, under the shower, getting ready for my date with the girl of my dreams.

I apply my cologne after coming out of the bedroom wearing a suit. I take my wallet and my car keys. I get out of my apartment, take out my car, and drive toward Mia's apartment. On the way, I buy a bouquet of flowers to make her happy. After driving for fifteen minutes, I reach her apartment.

I park my car and come out. After taking the flowers out, I go to her apartment door and ring the bell. Within a minute, Mia opens the door. My eyes get stuck on her. She looks gorgeous. Her beautiful eyes melt me. She smiles as she looks at me. Mia looks so ravishing right now that I am considering canceling the date and spending our time in her bed. I'm about to lose myself in her when I notice we're outside her door.

Clearing my throat, I hand her the flowers. She looks at them in surprise, like she did not expect me to bring flowers to her.

"You look gorgeous," I compliment her, my voice low, and she smiles. Her smile is so pretty that I do not have words to describe it. I give her my hand, and she takes it. I then lead her to my car, and help hold her door open as she gets in. I start driving to the surprise location.

We will arrive there soon. I park my car, and after getting out, I open the side of Mia's door. I give her a hand to pull her out, leading her toward the surprise. She gasps when she sees my surprise for her.

She turns toward me and says, "A date by the beach. Dominic, this is so pretty."

· · ·

I smile at her, "I'm so glad you like it. I did this for you. You love these kinds of dates, right?"

Mia looks at me and says, "Yes, I do. Thank you so much for giving me such a beautiful surprise!"

"Not as beautiful as you, baby girl," I say and look at her, staring into her eyes.

Mia looks down and blushes. I smile, looking at her red cheeks.

"Come, darling, I want to show you something." I lead her to the table set along the shore.

As I thought about where to bring Mia, I immediately thought about this beachside condo. This belongs to a friend of mine. It is right next to the beach and offers beautiful views of the water.

. . .

I pull the chair out, and Mia sits down. I pop open the wine and pour it out into the glasses. We pick them up and clink our glasses together. I take a sip and then remove the foil covers from the food I had catered.

After uncovering it, I serve some to Mia and some to myself. When I finally look up after doing it, I find Mia looking at me. She is staring at me with her hand on her chin. When I raise my brow at her, she smiles at me. I smile back.

"Eat up, baby girl."

She blushes again at my intimate nickname for her and nods. I could get used to seeing her across the table from me every day. I've never been so smitten by someone before. We both start eating, casually saying something about ourselves here and there. I even tell her about my family. She listens to everything intently.

I tell her some jokes to make her laugh. Tonight, I decided to show her I am not only a broody person obsessed with his past. I want to be free of all that. I can be romantic and fun.

After eating, I play some music on my phone.

"I'd love to dance with you," I say, and I ask for her hand. She first looks at me like I have grown another head. "Come on, would you dance with me, please?"

She shakes her head and smiles at me amusingly. Mia then puts her hand in mine and stands up. I keep my hand on her waist; she puts her arms around my neck. We both move to the slow tune. While dancing, she suddenly keeps her head on my chest, and my breath hitches in my throat. We both move slowly as the intoxicating air surrounds us. The fairy lights that are strung along the beach illuminate Mia's face. We both look at each other, and for the first time, Mia leans in to kiss me. She stands on her tippy toes, joins our lips, and kisses me. This kiss is not like others. It is sweet and full of love.

· · ·

I'm shocked that the word has come into my mind. *Love? Is that what I'm feeling?*

This time I let Mia take the lead, and I respond with the same sweetness. After our kiss, Mia looks down in shyness, and I laugh at the color of her cheeks. Listening to me laugh, her cheeks reddened. I hold her chin and make her look at me. We make eye contact with each other. Mia takes my hand in hers.

"Dominic?"

"Yes, sweetheart?" I reply, enjoying the sound of every term of endearment from my lips to her.

"It's probably obvious how much I like you. It happened so fast. You are still a mystery to me, but I am loving this mystery, and I hope you will not break my heart." She stares at me with honesty in her eyes, and I am stunned hearing her confession.

. . .

I hold her hand and say, "I have already fallen for you, and I promise you that you will not regret this decision. I'll never hurt you. You are mine now, just mine."

As I say this, I slam my lips onto hers and, while kissing her, I pick her up, and she wraps her legs around my waist. I lick her lips and bite them to enter her mouth. She moans a little. I suck one of her lips, and she sucks on mine. As the kiss goes on, I move towards the condo's door, pulling her inside. I keep my hands on her waist. We reach the kitchen counter, and I make her sit on the marble. I leave her lips and start kissing her neck. I bite her where her neck and shoulder blade meet.

"Ahh!" Mia moans.

I bite again, this time harder, listening to her moan. Then I press her breasts in my hands. Then she lifts off her dress over her head. I start kissing the valley between her breasts. Taking a hand at her back, I unhook her bra, and both her breasts come out as if someone has freed them. I make Mia lean on the counter and bring my mouth down on her nipple. After latching on to her nipple, I suck it till it becomes a small, peaked bud.

Mia keeps moaning, her hands in my hair, tugging tightly. When I become satisfied with one breast, I jump to the other one. The same is repeated with this breast. Done paying attention to her breasts, I kiss her stomach and move down. I take off her underwear and toss it. Her bare, wet pussy is in front of me. I do not wait for a second more and lick her wet folds without any warning. Moans and groans come out of Mia's mouth. I take two fingers and push them inside her warm center, fingering and sucking her together. I bring her to climax with my mouth, and with a huge moan, she releases her juices on my tongue.

Doing this, my pants tighten. My dick is too hard. So, without waiting, I unzip my pants and my dick springs out. Mia puts her hand on it and squeezes it. I coat my dick in her pussy juice, then enter in one straight push.

"Ah! Dominic!" shouts Mia.

. . .

I start going in and out, and I increase my speed as Mia screams. Within a few minutes, we both are riding the high together.

As I come into her, I keep my body on her, taking deep breaths. I can't imagine life without her.

Six

As The Danger Gets Closer

Mia

As the days' pass, the danger that Dominic's past poses continues to grow in my mind, and I find myself becoming more and more anxious as I come to terms with the reality of his situation. I can't seem to shake the feeling that danger lurks around every corner and that we are being watched. I love dating him. Our passion for each other is off the charts. He makes me feel like I am his favorite person in the world, and I relish how he dotes on me.

Each time a hint of his past comes up, those sweet moments feel tarnished. Things get exponentially worse a few days after we started dating. In spite of our best efforts, we have been found out and start to receive threatening phone calls and letters from unidentified individuals. We are constantly on the edge of our seats, always looking over our shoulders to see what's going on around us.

One particular night, as we are getting ready to close up the club, I hear a noise coming from the back alley. I turn to Dominic, my heart pounding with fear. "Did you hear that?" I ask, my voice barely above a whisper.

Dominic's expression hardens as he listens carefully. "Yeah," he said, his voice low and dangerous. "Stay here, and I'll go check it out."

Observing Dominic with his hand resting on the gun he keeps in his apartment that he'd moved to the bar, I watch him walk toward the back door of the building. However, despite knowing he is more than capable of handling whatever danger lies ahead of him, I still find myself worrying about him. He is ready to pounce at the unseen danger.

He went out to see what was out there while I waited inside, crouched with my knees pressed up against my chest, keeping a watchful eye on what he does. I try to stay calm and make sure I don't cause any noise.

The feeling of fear is running through my mind as I wait in the club. I feel as if my heart is about to burst out of my chest as I hear the sounds of a scuffle outside.

Finally, after what feels like an eternity, the door to the club opens, and Dominic walks in, his shirt stained with blood. "What happened?" I ask, my voice shaking with fear.

"Nothing for you to worry about," Dominic said, his voice hard. "I took care of it."

There is clearly something wrong, but I have not pursued the matter, even though I can tell it's serious. There is no doubt in my mind that Dominic will tell me if I need to know. I've never had anyone to support me, so I would like to support Dominic through thick and thin. His word is the only thing I can trust at this point, and he seems to be trying hard to prove himself to me.

The feeling of unease that has settled over me cannot be shaken off. In spite of the fact that I am aware that we are in the middle of a dangerous situation, I am not sure whether we will be able to make it out safely.

Over the next few days, the danger continues to

escalate. We receive more threats, and there were several attempts to break into the club. Each time, we manage to fend off the danger, thanks to our combined efforts.

One night, as we are leaving the club, a group of men ambush us. I have no choice but to fight with them, as they are all armed and dangerous, and there is not much we can do about it.

As the men close in on us, I feel a surge of fear and adrenaline. I know that this is it, that we are fighting for our lives.

It wasn't until a few minutes later that police officers appear on the scene out of nowhere. They had been tipped off about the attack by an anonymous source and had come to help us. They begin to investigate the situation, their presence allowing us to make it out alive.

But even as we celebrate walking out of the scuffle, I know that the danger isn't over. There are still people out there who want to harm us, who might even want to see us dead.

Over time, the threats grow less frequent, and the danger begins to feel like it will fade away. And finally, we are able to put the past behind us and move forward together. We are still keeping our heads down, too afraid to trust we are in the clear. I'm glad we can focus more on each other, now. Our relationship feels strong, and I want to keep it that way.

A few days after the attack, I realize just how much we have been through. But through it all, we have never given up on each other. We will never lose faith in each other. And in the end, that's what makes all the difference.

The club is gradually returning to normal as things settle down a bit. We are able to focus on the work that we do and on each other rather than constantly looking over our shoulders at each other so that we can both be better at what we do and improve.

During that time, Dominic and I grow even closer to each other. It has been through our shared experience of fighting off danger and protecting each other that we have been able to establish a bond that I had never imagined would be possible. Gone is the cocky man I used to work for. In his place is a genuinely good guy. I can't believe I spent so much time working for him before the storm and judging him so harshly. Behind his braggadocios attitude was a whole lot of guilt. I'm seeing the real Dominic, now.

We spend more and more time together, both at work and outside of it. We talk about our hopes and dreams, our fears and insecurities. And despite our age difference and different backgrounds, we find that we have a lot in common.

One day, during lunch break, we start talking about our hopes and dreams for the future.

"I've always wanted to start my own business outside of bars and real estate. You know, something really professional and white-collar," Dominic says, looking down at his sandwich. "But I'm afraid I'll never have the guts to do it."

"I think that is a great idea. I'd love to help." I smiled at him, full of faith in his abilities.

He looked up at me, his eyes brightening. "You're right. Maybe we could start something together. We work well together."

And so, as we continued to work on the project, we started brainstorming ideas for a new business venture. It was exciting to share our dreams and aspirations with each other and to support each other in pursuing them.

As Dominic and I were sitting on the couch in Dominic's apartment one evening, I looked at him and said, "You know, I never thought I would be with someone like you."

Dominic is staring at me with a small smile playing at the corners of his mouth as he looks at me. In response to this question, he asks, "What do you mean?"

"I mean," I said, "you're so different from anyone I've ever been with before. You're older, you're wealthy, and you've had a much different life than I have."

Dominic nods slowly, understanding in his eyes. "I know," he said. "But that doesn't mean we can't be together. We have a connection, Mia. And that's what matters. Also, I promise you I would never let my past get to you. I know there are still doubts in your heart that you don't let me see, but I will do everything I can to prove it to you."

I smile, feeling a warm feeling spread through my chest. "You're right," I said. "I'm just grateful that we found each other. And I'm trying my best to trust you."

Dominic leans in, his hand finding mine. "Me too," he said, his voice low and rough.

He leans in very close to me, and we kiss. The way this kiss makes me feel is something I can't explain. I'm breathless and feel like I would suffocate if I lost him.

His hands keep moving all over my clothes making me hotter and hungrier for him. I take off my shirt, and he unhooks my bra and starts playing with my breasts. I'm still not ready to let go of the kiss, but he pulls away, leaving me wanting more. I pounce on him, but he keeps me at bay, and I'm on my back with him on top of me.

He comes in for another kiss, and we forget everything else. I take off his shirt, unbutton his pants and rake my fingers over his body, starting from his neck and slowly making their way to his manhood, which is now erect and inviting. I wrap my legs around his waist and pull him closer, but he jerks away panting and takes his pants off and yanks at mine till I'm lying there exposed.

He swoops back in on top of me and kisses my lips, then trails a line of kisses on my body leading to my labia that he bites, making me moan so loud I am afraid someone might have heard it. However, he isn't done with me just yet as he moves back up, still between my legs, and kisses me while pushing his dick deep inside me. I feel like I'm full to the brim. His presence feels like a piece of me that was missing, and now it is finally attached to me. My mind lingers on his past, but I try to push it aside and focus on the now. I want to trust him completely.

He starts moving, and I follow his rhythm. We keep at it till we reach the point of pleasure and erupt in sweet ecstasy, both of us panting and feeling relaxed in each other's company.

There is a sense of accomplishment that I feel as we

sit here together in the quiet of the night, knowing that we can build a brighter future together. There have been times of hardship and uncertainty on my part, and I know we can come out from this experience stronger than ever before.

It is with complete confidence that I lean in to kiss Dominic and I know that we are going to remain united for the rest of our lives. As a result of our fight for each other, we have won for now, but we still have a long way to go. There is only one thing that really matters, and our love is it.

Seven

Jake!

Dominic

Mia works magically behind the counter normally, but today, she seems frozen by someone's presence among the other patrons at the Miami Club. I sit close to the bar, sipping on my beer, in earshot range, when a tall, well-dressed individual approaches her.

He greets Mia with a, "hello there" as his eyes travel all over her body. "You look nice."

I can already feel anger boil inside me.

Mia puts on a fake grin while attempting to maintain her distance. She is well aware that he is a source of trouble, and she resolves not to participate in any more of his antics.

She questions him as she stands there with her arms crossed over her chest, "Jake, what are you doing here? How did you find me?"

"I simply wanted to see you," he states as he moves closer to her while maintaining eye contact. "I miss you, Mia. Can we talk?"

Mia shakes her head in disapproval. "Jake, I do not believe it is a smart move at all. Right now, I'm with someone else."

Jake peeks over her shoulder and spots me observing them from across the table. This causes his eyes to narrow, and he frowns. He questions, "Who is that guy?"

Mia says firmly, "It has nothing to do with you and your concerns."

Jake moves his body closer to her. "Mia, come on, now. Together, you and I had a great time. Don't try to convince me that you've forgotten about the nights we spent together."

I can tell Mia is becoming more and more disgusted. "Jake, you had an affair with another woman. You destroyed my heart beyond repair. It is not something I have forgotten."

The look on Jake's face becomes gloomy. "I made a mistake, Mia. I am sorry. I still love you. I know that you are still in love with me, too." He leans a lot closer to her.

Mia shakes her head again. "Jake, you have zero knowledge of my personal life. I'm telling you, you need to leave before I contact the police or security."

This is my cue. I have had enough of this guy. I quickly stand up and arrive at Mia's side without a word. My face says it all. I wait until this Jake guy makes eye contact with me.

"No need for the police to be involved, eh? Dominic here," I say and offer a handshake. "Owner of this club. I see you are having some trouble. Let's talk outside, alone, shall we?" I say in an assertive voice.

Jake recoils, his eyes becoming tight. I can tell he feels intimidated by me. "Alright. But Mia, I will return. When that time comes, I will make sure you don't forget the good times we had together."

Mia stands as if she is petrified, and gloominess appears on her face as Jake turns and walks out of the club after he finishes speaking.

I am aware that she is hiding something from me,

but I don't want to push her into telling the truth about who this guy once was to her. So, I walk behind the bar and start serving drinks until her nerves calm down.

After a few minutes, Mia walks up to me, cupping her fingers. "Hello," she greets me, with a trace of instability in her voice. "We need to talk."

I raise my eyes to gaze at her, a look of worry appearing. "Mia, what's the matter? Everything all right?"

"Thank you for getting him off my back earlier," she says sincerely.

She takes a long breath before updating me about Jake's visit. She goes on to describe how he has made attempts to get her back and how he had threatened her when she did not give in to his demands. She hadn't seen him since they broke up over nine months ago, and the last thing she expected was for him to show up at her workplace. She realizes that he has been stalking her.

While I listen, my face gradually becomes more serious. I speak to her in a forceful tone, assuring her, "I won't let Jake hurt you, Mia. Don't worry about anything; I'll handle it," I say with disgust in my tone. I can feel my anger raging—the audacity of this guy to show up and torment Mia.

On the other hand, Mia has a wave of relief that

sweeps over her. She is aware that I am a powerful and competent guy, so she decides to put her faith in me to safeguard her.

She expresses her gratitude by patting my hand and saying, "Thank you. If it weren't for you, I don't know what I would do."

As I glance at her, my eyes take on a more compassionate expression. "Mia, you don't need to be concerned about anything. I am and will always be here for you."

As I look into Mia's eyes, I experience a warm sensation that travels to the center of my chest. I am well aware of how fortunate I am to have her in my life, and I have solemnly pledged to myself that I won't let any harm come to her.

Because of Jake, Mia continues to be on edge throughout the night. But she ultimately comes to a place of relative mental comfort when the shift ends. She is able to breathe a sigh of relief after realizing that I am keeping an eye out for her.

I escort Mia to my apartment as the club closes for the night, with my arms slung over her shoulder. Usually we don't sleep over at each other's places too often to try to keep some boundaries since we work together every day. But tonight she insists on staying at my place.

I am still on edge since Mia's ex-boyfriend has been up to the club unexpectedly. With all that has transpired between them, I am afraid of losing her, and I can't help but wonder whether she still cares for her ex. We are returning to my apartment, and I feel nervous.

Mia walks straight to the bathroom to take a shower, leaving me to reflect alone. I inhale deeply and make an effort to relax. I have to put my confidence in Mia, but I can't get rid of the uneasy feeling.

I sit on the sofa, remembering my life. I am not proud of my past involvement in criminal activity. It has taken me a long time to break free from my past. Yet the guilt still plagues me, especially at certain moments, but whenever I am with Mia, I feel all my past worries evaporate. I can't stand the thought of losing her.

So, how should we deal with you? Mr. Jake? I start to ponder, and a brilliant idea pops up in my brain. "That should take care of him." I punch in a few numbers and call my friend, Shawn. I explain the situation and hang up the phone with a grin.

Mia walks out, and I can see that Mia is still distressed as she walks toward me. I kneel down beside her and inquire into her feelings sympathetically.

"I can't believe he turned up like that," Mia murmurs, her voice tinged with exasperation. "After all this time, he believes he can simply walk back into my life."

I grasp her hand and give her a gentle, comforting squeeze. "You shouldn't fret about him. I already took care of him."

Mia gives me a look of shock, and before she can speak further, I pull Mia close to me. She leans in for a tender kiss on the lips. "Sure, if you say so."

And the next moment, my tongue caresses her as I place my arms over her shoulders, and she opens her mouth to me. I insert my tongue inside, giving her the feel of a sudden, passionate kiss. Her lips are on my lips, softly and tenderly kissing me; they are so gentle that I almost think a breeze is kissing me. It's so smooth and subtle, but it is enough to turn me on, creating heat between us. She kisses me as I have a taste once, twice, and I know there will never be enough.

Suddenly, she starts kissing me more intensely and passionately than ever before.

I gently touch her and whisper, "I hope your stress has vanished."

"Yes!" she replies as I move my hand over her shoulders. She pleads with me not to stop.

She reciprocates my touch before exerting more pressure and kissing me repeatedly while I cup her face in my hands. As our lips entwine, this kiss seems to be an assurance of tomorrow. Mia and I are in heat now, as if one kiss will make everything better for us.

I grab her body and bring her closer to me. She takes a step back as I grip her waist. Before kissing her again, I take a breather. She begins unbuttoning my shirt and kissing me all the way down to my underwear. As she gets to the final button on my jeans, she yanks them down. My dick emerges in front of her when I remove my underpants. She likes my length. I grab her hair and thrust it into her mouth gently as she sucks. Then I help her stand and pull on her towel, showing her beautiful breasts. My thumbs brush across her nipples. I tower above her, our lips just touching.

I massage her jaw, neck, and breasts. My fingertips tease her nipples, causing her to exhale. I stroke her hair and then push her back onto the bed. I stroke her clitoral region. I circle it while kissing her thighs.

"So wet," I mumble. "Ready?" I say as my fingers brush across her clit, and everything blurs for her. She can't stop the shaking that starts in her stomach and travels up her spine. Her hips collide with mine, and she lets out a gasp. When waves of pleasure rush through her, she lets out a moan. She can't seem to stop pressing her lips up onto my mouth. I move up her body, kissing her lips. We continue to kiss as my body reacts powerfully. Her pussy becomes wetter by the minute. She wants me more and more as we kiss. I take a step back from her and remove my shirt. I slide my dick into her and run my fingertips over her breasts and stomach before climaxing with one last thrust.

After cleaning ourselves, we sleep, feeling safe for the night, all worries about gangs and ex-boyfriends forgotten.

Eight

Mr. & Mrs. Bentley

Mia

I couldn't believe it when Dominic announced two days ago that he needed to take a short trip to visit his parents. When he had asked me to join him, my first thought was that he just wanted to swoop me up and take me far away from my creepy ex. Whatever the reason, I'm excited. Meeting his parents is a huge deal, and I hope it goes smoothly.

I am overcome with wonder as I leave the cab in

New York City and see the city's many gigantic buildings for the first time. This is the city that never sleeps, the place where dreams are created and destroyed simultaneously. And now, I am here with Dominic to meet his family and learn more about Dominic's background.

I know that Dominic is not too fond of his parents. They are super rich, and he is going to be seeing them after a long time of avoiding them. But the question "why" has been bugging me the whole trip. Why does he want me to meet his parents so suddenly?

It's as if Dominic can read minds. "I see that look on your face, baby girl. I know what you want to ask me."

"Oh, really? You're a mind reader, now?" I tease him and laugh.

"I guess we'll see. You are probably wondering why I asked you to join me and meet my parents. Well, I feel that it's time. You are important to me." He takes a pause to absorb my smile and continues. "And, they have been requesting me to come see them for the longest time, but I always ignored their messages. They have something big to talk to me about and I've been avoiding it. But this time, I thought I could introduce you!" He plants a kiss on my lips. "I told you, I'm done running away from my past."

I can't help but feel a mix of pride and anxiety about Dominic's reply. As we go through the bustling streets with the other people, my mind starts to flood with more questions. What if his parents don't take a shine to me? What if I don't feel like I belong in their expensive and luxurious lifestyle? Yet, as soon as we enter Dominic's family house, all of my concerns disappear for the moment.

Dominic's family home is a vast mansion that is tall and narrow, typical of the city. As I enter the front doors, I am greeted by a large lobby with marble flooring and a diamond, glittering chandelier. The walls are covered with oil paintings of Dominic's ancestors, their stern expressions following me as I move around the house.

The home is decorated in an old-money, classic-elegance manner. Ornate and built of expensive wood, the furniture includes soft velvet padding and elaborate carvings. The grandeur of it all makes me feel a bit frightened, as if I am an outsider peering in on a world I can never fully be a part of.

The rooms are open and airy, with high ceilings and huge windows allowing plenty of natural light. I stroll along the corridors, appreciating the exquisite plasterwork on the ceilings.

We meet a butler as soon as I wander where I am

not supposed to, and he leads us to a large living room, where Dominic's parents are already sitting and waiting for us to arrive.

A grand piano stands in one corner of the living room, flanked by velvet armchairs and a plush couch. I am taken aback by the beauty of it all, and I wonder how it must feel to grow up in such luxury.

I can't help but feel out of place. But I am determined to enjoy the experience and learn more about Dominic, the guy I am falling for, even if it means venturing outside of my comfort zone.

But the real challenge is about to start. I am being confronted by Dominic's parents. I am feeling intimidated by the refined and cultured pair. They are dressed in designer clothes and speak with accents that hint at a life of privilege and sophistication.

"Hello, Mother. Hello, Father. Good to see you. Hello to you as well, Harold," Dominic says. An aged man standing beside him gives a soft smile when he greets him, telling me that Harold must have been a butler of Dominic's since childhood.

Dominic sits beside me and clears his throat, but his mom interrupts him. She jolts up in her expensive dress and walks towards him. I realize even the way she walks is refined.

"My child, how long has it been since you came to visit us? This is your home, after all!" she speaks, pecking him on both cheeks.

I can tell that Dominic is already irritated as he says tightly. "Please, Mom. I am not a child anymore. Also, I have someone with me. Someone really important to me." He points at me.

My body is stiffer than a pole as both of his parent's gazes lock on to me.

"And who might she be?" asks Dominic's father. His voice is deep and assertive, just like his son's.

"Mia, this is my father, Arthur, and my mother Lisa. Father, Mother, this is Mia Farrino." Dominic introduces me, and I greet them with a smile.

The Bentleys are well-known philanthropists, prominent business owners with stakes in several firms, and active managers of numerous organizations. It's remarkable to learn that Mr. Bentley supported himself by doing odd jobs when he was in college, and Mrs. Bentley was a waitress.

They teamed together after getting married and started investing in undervalued businesses using a value-investment strategy. They concentrated on businesses that the market had undervalued and purchased shares of such businesses below their true worth. Their perseverance and passion were rewarded as their company developed over time and finally became worldwide.

Due to their prosperity, they have significant stock in many corporations, often travel for business meetings, and are happy parents to Dominic.

His mother starts walking towards me, judging me with her hazel eyes. I can already tell Lisa Bentley has played a significant role in the success of the Bentleys.

"Hello, Mrs. Bentley. Nice to meet you," I greet her with a warm smile.

"Oh, dear. Please. Away with the formalities. After all, you are the reason Dominic decided to see us after all these years. We can't be more thankful," she says and smiles. "Let's eat before the food gets cold."

As the conversation progresses, Dominic's parents start to stun me with stories from his childhood.

"I assumed that Dominic's upbringing in a luxurious family would have resulted in him being a spoiled and pampered child. But he is a boss that has all of my respect," I say and lock my eyes with Dominic. He smiles back at me in appreciation.

I quickly come to my senses and wonder if I spoke too much, but the chuckles of his parents give me a sense of relief.

On the other hand, I also know that his parents always used to keep a distance from him and were often more concerned with their work than they were with Dominic.

His father turns his focus to Dominic. "Dominic, my boy, we are really sorry for our part in how things were just before you left. After you left, we reflected on our situation, and our priorities as parents have transformed. We have started to place a higher value on family than on everything else in our lives. We didn't know how much we had lost out on or how much we had taken for granted until you went off, leaving this house empty. I know time cannot be reversed, but we want you to know we are proud of the man you have become. You are welcome here at any time."

I am in utter shock his father broached the topic. He waits for his son's response.

Dominic's face softens at his father's words, sensing sincerity in them. Although his family cannot heal his wounds, they can fill them, instead. He sits back and nods his thanks at his father. His mom takes the opportunity to inquire more about me and questions my aspirations.

I feel intimidated by her questions, but Dominic supports me at every query, telling stories about my artwork and my job as a bartender. His parents seem impressed by my talent and ambition.

As we sit together, swapping tales, I can see the love and pride in Dominic's parents' eyes. Even though they were not there throughout his youth, they are present now, trying to make up for lost time and demonstrating their love and support for their son in every way that they possibly can.

After dinner, Dominic asks me to take a stroll through the small back garden, to which I agree. Inevitably the topic of Jake comes up.

"Dominic, he hasn't called me or texted. Whatever you did, it worked," I say with gratitude.

"Jake? I told Shawn, my friend, to dig up his past. It turns out he had turned to a bunch of illegal crap. I just wanted him to know that his shady dealings weren't a secret, and that he could get into a lot of trouble if he didn't stay away," he says softly. "Is that okay, how I handled it?"

I thank him by giving him a kiss which he wasn't expecting. Relief floods his face.

"So. Your parents welcomed you back into their lives. I'm so happy for you."

He smiles. "Yes. I want you to er... explore this place a bit more," he says evasively.

"Sure," I reply, knowing he is considering giving

his family a second chance and wants to experience what he missed.

As I gaze into his eyes, I am aware that there is still much more to discover about him and more for me to adore about him.

Nine

The Café

Dominic

I have been in New York with Mia for several days. She has been watching the way I live my life. I am a billionaire here, and my family owns the most expensive properties around the city. We are a known name. Although I am not fond of this wealth, ultimately, it does belong to me. I brought Mia to my family's house. When I first entered the house with her, I'd thought my parents were not there. I had rolled my eyes. Of course, why would they be there?

Why would they care that their only son had come back after so many years? I was glad to discover I was wrong, and that they were welcoming to both Mia and me.

After introducing Mia, I can tell my parents respect her. Their approval gives me the extra boost I need to consider their offer. I haven't talked to Mia about it, but after our time on the town today, I plan to. I haven't made up my mind, yet, and I want her input. We are upstairs in my room and Mia says she would die for a snack. As she makes for the door, I laugh and tell her that the butlers will bring up anything she needs, and she should rest before I take her out and show her a few of my favorite sights. We've been so busy with my parents, lately, that I haven't taken her out just the two of us, yet.

I remind her that she does not need to lift a finger as long as she is here. Anything she needs, all she has to do is order it, and it will get done. Then I kiss her and give her tight little booty a swat.

She laughs and goes to freshen up. After fifteen minutes, she comes out wearing a bathrobe. Seeing her with wet hair and wrapped in a silky robe, my eyes shine with lust. I stand up and stalk towards her. She moves back and soon hits the wall. I walk towards her like she is the only thing I care about in the world, licking my lips in desire. Reaching her, I slide a hand around her waist and pull her towards me.

She gasps. "Dominic, wh… what are you doing? Your parents are downstairs."

I keep my hand in the crook of her neck. Taking in her fresh soap fragrance, I lick her neck a little.

"No one will hear. This is my time with you." Saying this, I bite her on the neck. She gasps. I pick her up in my hands and throw her on the bed. Taking my shirt off, I go on top of her. I slam my lips on her. Sucking and biting her lips, I pull the rope off her robe, and it comes undone. As I see her naked body, my dick tightens in my pants. So, without waiting for any more protests, I start feasting on her breasts. I take her nipple in between my fingers and pull it, causing her to moan. Listening to her moaning, I pull even harder. Then I start to play with it, pleasuring her. Nuzzling my face into her breasts, I suck, bite, and lick her. Mia's hands scratch my back as she pulls me more into her. Mia keeps gasping and moaning breathily. My control soon slips away, so I take off my jeans. I turn Mia around doggie style, and without warning, I push my length completely inside of her. I take hold of her hair and thrust inside her tight pussy.

She moans my name loudly, "Ahh, Dominic."

Soon Mia rides on my dick, but I am not done. I

keep thrusting when I feel close. I hold her breasts and push much faster. Within a minute, I release into her. We both separate, and I lay down on my back. Looking at her, I smile. Every time with her feels like the first time. She sits up and pulls the robe around her before going into the bathroom to get ready for our time out in the city.

Soon after, someone knocks on the door. I order them to come in, and the butler steps in.

He has a bottle of champagne and some exotic fruit and fresh juice. "You requested refreshment," he says primly. With a slight bow, he leaves.

I take Mia's hand and make her sit. We both munch on the fruit and enjoy some champagne. Once we are done, I ask Mia to finish getting ready, as I am taking her to get appetizers and show her around. She nods, looking happy. I go inside to shower. When I come out, I find Mia sitting on the dressing chair. She finishes doing her makeup and stands, looking at me. "How am I looking?" she asks, twirling in her pretty white, short dress.

"Beautiful," I reply. "Do you want to ditch the outing and spend the day in bed?" I waggle my eyebrows at her.

She laughs while listening to me and pushes me away. I laugh at her and say, "Okay, okay. Let's go." I hold her hand and we go down the stairs to the front entryway.

I am excited to take Mia out. As we sit in the car and drive away towards the café, I look at her. Her red lips excite me, so I turn her face and brush my lips on hers, kissing her deeply while the driver drives the car.

Before we can go any further, Mia stops me, pointing at the driver. I dismiss her signal, panting. I hold her chin and go back to kissing her. Mia stops me again when the car halts. The driver informs me that we are there. I open the car door and step out. Moving to the other side, I open Mia's door and give her a hand. As she comes out, we start heading towards the cafe. We are about to enter when the paparazzi gather. They start clicking their cameras and calling out my name. They also focus on Mia and on my hand, which is around her waist.

They start chanting my name, asking me questions about who the girl with me is, whether I am back here to stay, where I have been these years, whether I am getting married, and many more. They keep asking me questions, but I do not reply and move inside with Mia. The café staff stops them from coming inside.

The staff shows us to our seats, and I pull a chair out of the table for her, and Mia takes a seat. I sit in my seat. I take a look at Mia and realize that she is not speaking at all.

I stare at her, and when she still does not pay attention, I snap my fingers in front of her, which startles her. She looks at me, and I raise an eyebrow, asking, "Mia, darling, are you fine? Is everything all right?"

Mia nods and replies, "Everything is fine. It is just that the paparazzi outside really shocked me. I never knew you were so famous. I mean, they were asking so many questions. This is weird to me."

I chuckled, listening to her. "Oh, darling, this may be unusual for you, but it's the unfortunate reality of my family's name. You have already seen my wealth. Since my parents own so much in the city and I am their only son, these people run behind me. They are always present wherever I am. It is difficult to process at the start. I used to hate it as well; however, you get used to it. It is like a part of my life."

I tell Mia, and she scrunches her nose after listening to me intently, "How do you even live like that? How can you be under constant scrutiny? Whatever you are doing, they are aware of it. Does it not make you feel weird? How do you manage all of this? I got so uncomfortable out there."

I shrug my shoulders and say, "There is nothing to

manage; you will soon become used to it. Come on, darling! Let us order something."

I call the waiter and order all the specialties. We talk to each other until our food comes. Once the food is here, we dig in.

"Mmm," Mia moans. "This is yummy."

I smile at her. After we are done, I pay the bill. Outside we are greeted by the paps again. When I notice this, I grab Mia and rush to the car. We sit, and Mia keeps her head on my shoulder. The driver drives the car, and Mia takes a deep breath. The rest of our time is fun. We drive around the city, and I point out the historic buildings to her.

Once reaching home, my mother welcomes us. She informs us that we are going to have a private dinner to get to know Mia some more and then a welcome party. All of the influential people in my family's social circles will be present. The media is also going to be there. She is going to tell everyone that I will be overtaking every-thing in the family business.

I remember then that I was planning to tell Mia, but hadn't managed to do so, yet. Her blunt words shock me, and before I can muster up something, I feel Mia staring at me. As Mia hears about the media being here, she looks at me with a worried expression.

Leaving the room quietly, she walks upstairs to my room and closes the door.

I look at my mother and say, "She is going to need a little time to adjust."

My mom replies, "I understand. Our lifestyle is a lot for most people to become used to."

I open my door and find Mia standing near the window. I hug her from behind. She turns and says, "Dominic, I need to talk to you."

Realizing that her tone is serious, I clear my throat and ask, "Yes? Go on, my love."

She holds my hand and says, "Dominic, I understand that you are wealthy and live a glamorous life. But I am not used to this life. I am a very simple person, and being in the limelight is quite difficult for me. I get uncomfortable with this."

I look at her. "Mia, dear, this is my life. I cannot escape from it."

I take her hand and squeeze it. "My parents want me to take over running the family empire, all the investments. And I'd love to do it with you by my side."

Ten

The Welcome Home Party

Mia

I am in Dominic's house, in his room, and I am currently lying down with my eyes closed. I inhale and exhale continuously, taking deep breaths to calm myself down. We made it through a pleasant family dinner. Then he took me outside for a moment of privacy before the guests arrived for the welcome home party. He exerted is influence and only allowed one reporter in, and that was only for one hour. I kept to the shadows the whole time until most of the guests left.

I respect the hard work his family put in to reach the status they have. But I have decided this lifestyle just isn't for me. Dominic is taking a shower and taking a moment to consider my perspective. I know he is considering his parents' offer of taking over the family estate and all their holdings.

I am thinking about this, and my eyes get full of tears. My lips quiver. I close my eyes again, trying to calm myself again. Before I can cry, the door to the room opens, and Dominic comes in from his shower.

Looking at him, I turn my face around. I feel the bed dip. Dominic sits down and keeps his hand on my waist. Once I sit up, he takes my hand and assures me that he has my back and that we can leave the city the next day, returning home. There is no need to rush, and he doesn't have to take over his family's estate anytime soon. Relief floods my body and I relax.

He kisses me on my lips, sweetly taking his time and sucking them. He uses his tongue to enter my mouth, and I give him a chance by opening my mouth.

We both play with our tongues roaming in our mouths. After kissing each other for quite a while, we separate, and I smile, looking at him. He brings his hand towards my face and traces his finger along my cheek. I close my eyes, feeling his touch. He takes his finger down to my neck, then to my breasts, and down. He then holds my face and kisses me again, this time not with sweetness but with lust. He kisses me hard and fast and pushes me onto my back. I reciprocate with the same adrenaline. I put my hand on his neck, pushing him more into me.

Leaving my lips all red, he moves towards my neck, where he starts kissing and biting. He sucks on some spots, which are my weak points, and it makes me moan.

He then moves toward the valley of my breasts. He kisses my breasts on top of my shirt. I turn him on his back. I take my shirt off and kiss him on the face. I take my hands to his t-shirt and take it off. His intimidating body welcomes me. I start kissing his biceps, moving to his torso. I trace his tattoo with my lips while licking at it, taking my sweet time.

Soon, Dominic will be unable to bear the torture because he holds my hair and turns me on my back. He unhooks my bra and makes my breasts free. He gets on to them like a starved caveman, biting, sucking, and licking them. I moan, feeling the pressure. I wind my fingers in his hair, tugging. He sucks my breasts until he is satisfied. After he leaves them, he moves down toward my stomach, kissing my navel.

Licking his lips, he moves down. Opening the button of my jeans, he slides them off. I am wearing lace panties. He puts his hand in my pants and says, "You are already so wet, baby girl. You are so excited."

He takes off my pants and pushes two digits inside me. I moan. "Yes," I say, and he starts fingering me in and out. He adds another digit and fingers me hard and fast. He takes his jeans off, spreads my legs, and enters me without warning. His length fills me up. I moan, feeling full.

He starts thrusting in and out of me without any mercy; he fucks me so hard that I see stars in my eyes.

He keeps fucking me until I am very close. But he does not let me come. He keeps thrusting until he is about to come, then he speeds up, and soon we both come undone. I lift my hips to ride our high together.

He falls on me when he is done. Taking his dick out, he falls onto the bed. Before I can say anything, he gets up and goes to the bathroom. He comes out a minute later, picks me up, and takes me in for a bath. I look at him, and he puts me into the bubble bath and gets inside himself. I rest my back on his chest, content.

He takes a deep breath before he says, "Mia, I want to say something." I look at him and say, "Yes?"

He looks at me in my eyes and says, "Mia, I love you. You are my everything. You brighten my day, and

I cannot imagine my life without you." He looks so vulnerable right now, confessing his love to me. I hug him, feeling happy about the confession.

"I love you too, Dominic. You have my heart."

Dominic smiles and hugs me.

Eleven

Returning To The Club

Dominic

I realize that Mia is unable to adjust to my environment, so I take her back to where both of us belong to get back to our routine. I realize at her age, Mia is only comfortable in her routine within her comfort zone, and I never want to pressure her too far out of it. Our relationship is still new, and we need time to grow together. In any case, I do not want things to be difficult for her. I want to prove to be a good partner for her as we move beyond my past and into a bright future.

I try to prove that I am fully committed to her, and

our relationship and she can trust me. She says she does, even knowing the worst part of me. I decide to make things beautiful for her.

Both of us settle in back at home and start our duties in the Miami Club. Mia and I also try to sort out all the things that both of us think still stand in the way of a future together.

I tell her that I have learned the only thing that is most important in life, other than love, is respect. The one who gives, gains back. Both of us agree. Things are going great when I learn that the gang leader wants to meet me.

I take this as a normal meeting because I am still responsible for meeting the leader when he calls on me. I had no idea that this meeting would be my last.

The gang's muscle man they sent walks silently into the club on a slow afternoon. With a single nod of his head, I get the message. I look for Mia to tell her, but don't see her. I assume she's in the kitchen. Silently, I follow the guy out front and into a van. It's routine to be taken to the gang leader. He rarely makes a public appearance. My guess is, he's wanted for quite a lot by the police. Being identified is too risky for him.

After a short drive, the van stops, and I can see a deserted warehouse in front of me. I'm a little taken aback because I cannot see anyone there. The big, muscled man takes me into the warehouse. It's dark and smells like mold. He stands there, arms folded. A little confused, I do the same. My sixth sense is kicking up—something is wrong.

After a few moments of silence, I hear the screams of Mia. My mind jolts. What on earth is going on?

The gang leader strides into the room as if he is out on a Sunday stroll. His voice drips arrogance as he says, "Did you feel the pain and fear of losing someone you love?"

Reality hits me hard. After all these years, he is finally making good on his threats. I look at him and try to ask, "Where is Mia?"

He replies, "So, you are impatient to meet your girl. Okay! You want her alive or dead?"

"Tell me where she is," I say with gritted teeth. I never want to lose Mia. "Please. She has nothing to do with this. Please—let her go."

He laughs and says, "I am glad to see you know your place and are groveling, right in front of me."

Rage bubbles inside me. I try to run toward him to attack him, but he moves away and takes a gun out of his pocket.

"One more move, and your Mia, beautiful Mia, is dead," he says and smiles, laughing loudly.

"Your beef is with me, leave her. I am here to pay

off my dealings with you once and for all," I reply, my gaze sincere. If there is one thing I remember about this guy, he can smell a lie a mile away. The way to win him over is with the truth.

"Oh really, what are you offering?"

He waves his hand and some of his boys bring Mia in front of me. They've tied a bandana around her mouth. Her eyes look frightened.

"She is so beautiful. Isn't she, Dominic?" he says.

"Leave her, I am telling you leave her alone. What do you want from me?"

"Oh, Dommy boy, I don't want your parents' money. I just want what is owed to me. Gold. I want that gold. Then we can consider our dealings settled."

I gape at him. I haven't been back to that property in over a decade. How do I even know the gold is still there?

"The thing about gold is, you can't trace it like cash. But you know that, don't you? That's why you've been keeping it for yourself."

I shake my head. "Not true. How do I know when I tell you where it is that you will leave me alone, forever?"

"I'll give you a blood oath. You have no value to me. And you're too much of a straight guy now to snitch. Tell me where it is. If it's there, we're done."

I rattle off the address faster than a breath. He nods to the muscle who leaves without a word. I hope to God that it's still there.

Two hours go by. Neither Mia nor I speak with two guns pointed at us the whole time. The most I can do is give her an assuring nod. Finally, the muscle is back. He doesn't say a word, just gives the leader a look and walks back out.

The leader claps his hands together. "Well, well, well. Looks like your debt to our fine underground society is paid in full."

He reaches for a knife, ready for a blood oath.

"I am straight now, as you said. Let's shake hands on it and be done." There is no way I'm mixing my blood with his.

He smirks at me, gives my hand a stiff shake then his muscle pushes Mia towards me. I pull off the bandana. We both scramble to our feet, eager to leave and never come back.

The muscle allows us to sit in the van undisturbed as he drives us back to the bar. I don't breathe easy until he drops us off.

Twelve

His Promise to Me

Mia

I can't even remember how it happened. All I know is a hood was placed over my face and I was picked up and put into a van. When I was allowed to take it off, I was in an empty building with two of the most dangerous-looking people I have seen in my entire life.

That was when I screamed, and Dominic heard me. They didn't hurt me physically, but the emotional damage will take a while to get over. Now that we are finally safe in Dominic's apartment, floods of tears break loose.

He lets me cry and holds me close to make me feel good. He tells me that nothing like this is going to happen again as things are square between him and the gang. The offer of a blood oath means the leader's words will never be broken. We are safe. Telling me this, he looks at me and places a soft kiss on my forehead to make me feel that I am not alone and the two of us are now out of that situation.

I look at him with tears in my eyes. I have never been through such a life-threatening situation and have never seen such a dangerous gang in my life. I know they could have killed us.

Dominic looks into my eyes and holds my hand, saying, "I am so sorry, Mia. You were put in so much danger, all because of me." He drops his gaze down, guilt written across his handsome face.

His words about the blood oath make me believe that this is never going to happen again.

I hold his hand tightly and assure him, "I trust you. I trust your words. You know, I got so scared that I would never see you again. I never want to feel so alone. If you hadn't gone with them to the warehouse, I would be dead. Thank you, Dominic, for saving my life." Saying this, I put my head on his shoulder and hug him.

He places his hands on my back and tightly hugs

me, saying, "You are my world, and I promise to be with you forever and ever. Don't worry! I am never going to let you down."

One thing I realize about the alarming situation is that Dominic is the one who can do anything for me and is, no doubt, the right person for me. I decided to be in a relationship with him as I know he is never going to betray his word. This quality attracts me, and I decide to confess the depth of my love in front of him. I move a little back from his shoulders and hold his hand to tell him about the feelings I have for him.

He looks at me with curiosity as I hold his hand.

He asks me, "Is everything okay?"

He looks at me again, and I say, "Yes, it's completely okay." Remaining quiet for a few seconds, I add, "I never realized it before, but today I want to tell you that I have never felt the way I feel for you ever in my entire life. I respect you, and more than that, I love you. I don't want to date anyone else. Ever."

I look at him, but I do not have more words that can help me express my love for him.

He looks at me with soft eyes and says, "The first night both of us spent together, I already made some promises toward you. Maybe those were not verbal promises, but for me, those were the feelings that I am having toward you. They've grown so much since that night. That night I told myself that maybe you are the right person to give a relationship a try. I want to build a future with you. And eventually, I want to explore the idea of marriage." He locks his eyes onto mine.

Suddenly, he stands up and moves to the dresser near his bed. I watch curiously as he pulls out a small black box covered in soft velvet. He comes back to bed, eyes alight with love.

"I was planning to do this at a fancy restaurant on a date, but the moment feels right, now." He sits on the bed next to me and strokes my cheek. "You are the light of my life. You trust me and believe in me no matter what. I want to give this to you as a symbol of how much I love you. And, one day, when we are both ready, I want..."

I press my fingers on his lips, not wanting him to give everything away all at once. I smile at him as he opens the box to reveal a dainty promise ring with a blue stone the color of my eyes centered on the band. Tears fill my eyes as I realize how much love this man has for me.

"I promise to be here for you and to love you, Mia. Always."

He slides the ring on my finger as a token of his commitment to us. I am absolutely at a loss for words as I kiss him passionately.

Both of us remain quiet for a few seconds looking at each other and smiling. We know there is a big age gap between us, so he is wise to take things slow. I have tears in my eyes. This love is so deep and real for us. I am in love for the first time in my life. I have never had such feelings for anyone before, and the way he proved his love for me continues to melt my heart.

I know without a doubt that he is the one I am willing to be with my whole life.

I look at him and smile, and he takes my hand, saying, "You never need to worry about gangs, my family's estate, or anything. I am here for you forever and ever. This bond is not going to break, and I am going to prove it to you every single day."

I look at him with love shining in my eyes, and he hugs me tightly.

I tell him, keeping my head on his muscular chest, "I don't care now about anything... just us."

He gradually moves me a little away and places a soft kiss on my forehead, and then he places a kiss on my lips.

I look at him with a smile, and he says, "Mia, you are the most important and precious part of my life. I love you with my whole heart."

I know that he means it and that this is just the beginning of a long and beautiful love story.

Acknowledgments

To Sheena, my developmental editor.

You are a shining light that came to me at the perfect time. Without you, this would NEVER have been possible.

My deepest gratitude always.

I hope we have a lifelong working relationship with each other.

To all the coaches –

Thank you for your continued support!

Chapter Images: Pixaby.com/Prawny-1766270
Formatted by: Dawn Baca

About the Author

Kasia Kain has always been an avid reader and fell in love with contemporary romance books long ago.

She has always wanted to write books and now feels the time is right to bring her stories to life for you.

Raised on the West Coast but settled in the High Desert Valley's the calming of the mountains and the desert allow this author to reach out and touch so many with steamy romance novels.

There is nothing better than being able to just escape on the couch on a Sunday or on the beach or in a cabin and read to your heart's content.

Kasia sincerely hopes you enjoy book after book that she brings to you.